BOTS

DANGER ON THE BOTSBURG EXPRESS

by Russ Bolts

illustrated by Jay Cooper

LITTLE SIMON

New York London Toronto Sydney New Delhi

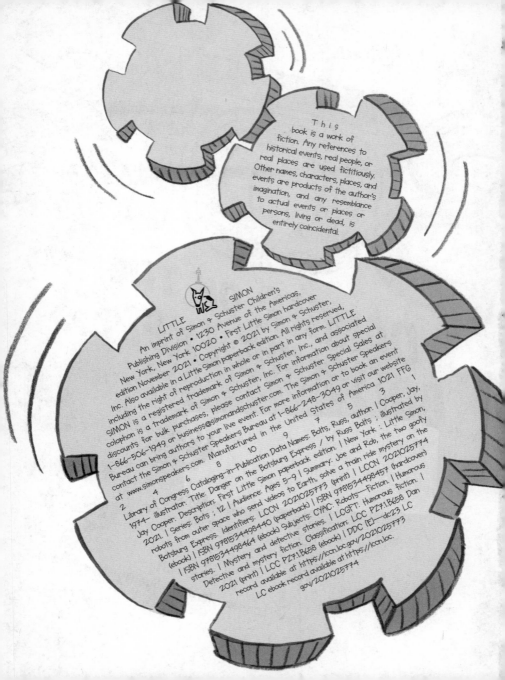

LITTLE SIMON

An imprint of Simon & Schuster Children's Publishing Division • 1230 Avenue of the Americas, New York, New York 10020 • First Little Simon hardcover edition November 2021 • Copyright © 2021 by Simon & Schuster, Inc. Also available in a Little Simon paperback edition. All rights reserved, including the right of reproduction in whole or in part in any form. LITTLE SIMON is a registered trademark of Simon & Schuster, Inc., and associated colophon is a trademark of Simon & Schuster, Inc. For information about special discounts for bulk purchases, please contact Simon & Schuster Special Sales at 1-866-506-1949 or business@simonandschuster.com. The Simon & Schuster Speakers Bureau can bring authors to your live event. For more information or to book an event contact the Simon & Schuster Speakers Bureau at 1-866-248-3049 or visit our website at www.simonspeakers.com. Manufactured in the United States of America 1021 FFG

2   4   6   8   10   9   7   5   3   1

Library of Congress Cataloging-in-Publication Data Names: Bolts, Russ, author. | Cooper, Jay, 1974- illustrator. Title: Danger on the Botsburg Express / by Russ Bolts ; illustrated by Jay Cooper. Description: First Little Simon paperback edition. | New York : Little Simon, 2021. | Series: Bots ; 12 | Audience: Ages 5-9 | Summary: Joe and Rob, the two goofy robots from outer space who send videos to Earth, solve a train ride mystery on the Botsburg Express. Identifiers: LCCN 2021025773 (print) | LCCN 2021025774 (ebook) | ISBN 9781534498440 (paperback) | ISBN 9781534498457 (hardcover) | ISBN 9781534498464 (ebook) | Subjects: CYAC: Robots—Fiction. | Humorous stories. | Mystery and detective stories. | LCGFT: Humorous fiction. | Detective and mystery fiction. Classification: LCC PZ7.1.B658 Dan 2021 (print) | LCC PZ7.1.B658 (ebook) | DDC [E]—dc23 LC record available at https://lccn.loc.gov/2021025773 LC ebook record available at https://lccn.loc.gov/2021025774

CONTENTS

A Funny Thing

8

PLATFORM 10101 3/4

13

18

CHAPTER 2

All Aboard

EXPRESS BOTSBURG EXPRESS BOTSBURG EXPRESS

STATION

23

THE DINING CAR HAS TWELVE DIFFERENT CHEFS READY TO COOK WHATEVER YOU WANT TO EAT.

THE SLEEPER CARS HAVE YOUR CHOICE OF BEDS, FROM SOFT TO FIRM TO UNDERWATER BEDS!

BUT WE ALL KNOW THAT THE CABOOSE IS THE WORST PART OF THE TRAIN. I MEAN, IT'S THE VERY LAST CAR, IT DOESN'T DO ANYTHING IMPORTANT, AND EVEN ITS NAME SOUNDS LIKE PEOPLE ARE BOOING AND HISSING AT IT. JUST LISTEN.

CA-**BOO-HISS!** CA-BOO-HISS! UGH, THAT CAR IS THE WORST!

LUCKY FOR US, THE CELEBRITY RIDERS ARE STARTING TO ARRIVE!

34

35

40

44

CHAPTER 4

The Quiet Car

And so Joe and Rob went looking for a car that would be perfect for them.

And the Safe Car was unbreakable.

UNBREAKABLE, YOU SAY?

YES, MAYOR. NOTHING GETS IN OR OUT WITHOUT MY KNOWING.

YOU SEE, I AM THE ONLY ONE WITH THE VAULT'S CODE.

WHAT'S THE CODE?

Joe and Rob went to the...

SHHH.

Joe and Rob went to the...

SHHH.

You know what? Joe and Rob can tell their own story. I'm out of here.

Isn't this nice? It gives me a chance to practice my riding, I mean, writing.

Well, we are riding on a train, so you are doing both!

Oh yeah! Ha! This is perfect. Nothing could go wrong now.

BOOM!

73

74

ZZZZ

GOLF

89

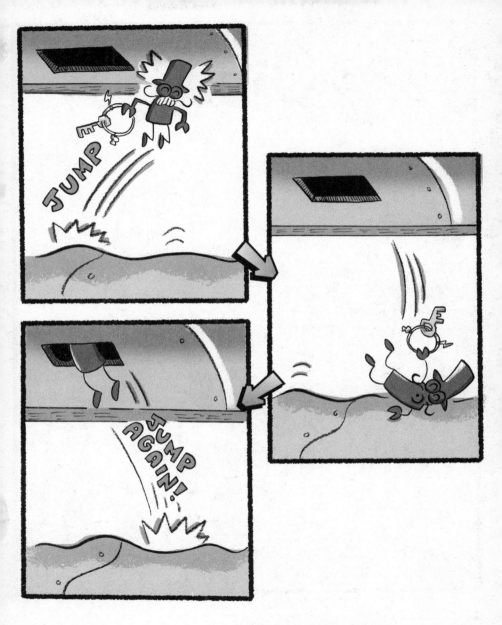

CHAPTER 8 The Chase

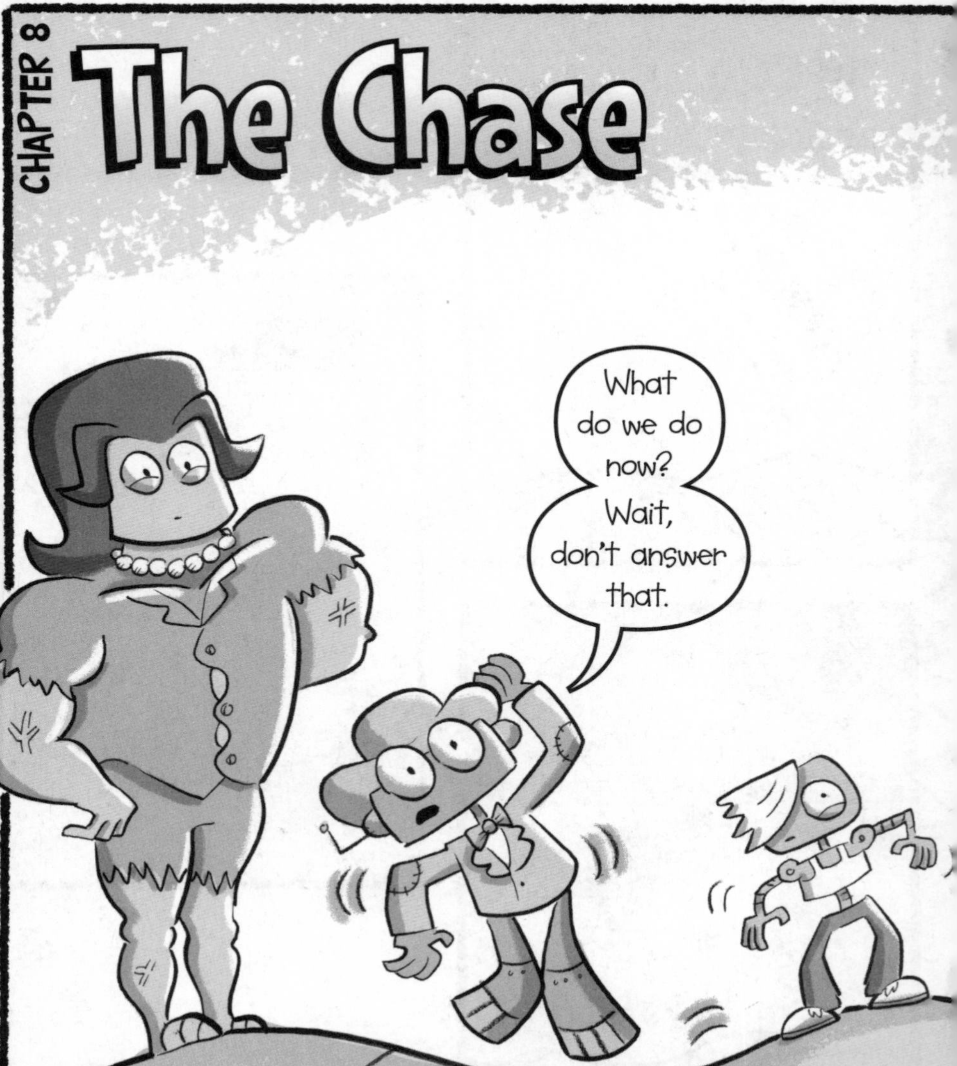

The Chew Chew Train

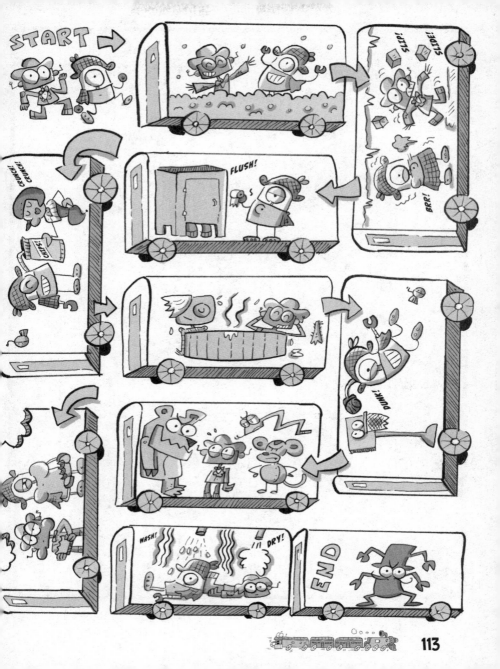

113

120

BLINK!

WAKE!

Rob, wake up, buddy. I think we fell asleep.

I just had the weirdest dream. You were there, and so was Tinny, but she didn't look like Tinny.

will be back with a new episode soon,
but in the **meantime**,
check out **JOE & ROB'S**
other adventures!

And don't forget to hit **LIKE**
at the bottom of the page!